ALSO BY KEITH BARNETT HUFF

<u>Children's Books</u>
DO KANGAROOS SWIM?
&
HERMAN THE PENGUIN

<u>Poetry</u>
The Flower is Neutral

SOME OTHER NEXT PAGE PUBLISHER'S BOOKS YOU WILL ENJOY BY RIDLEY BARNETT

SPRING-HEELED JACK or
THE TERROR OF LOUISVILLE PART I

FOR SALE BY OWNER

(revised edition)

FOR SALE
BY OWNER
(revised edition)

Original Short Story & Screenplay

KEITH BARNETT HUFF

NEXT PAGE *PUBLISHERS*
LOUISVILLE, KY
EST. 2018 ~

CONTENTS

FOREWORD

by Herschel Zahnd

A Culmination of Firsts

What you are holding is truly special. "A Culmination of Firsts." What do I mean by that? Well, glad you asked. When I met Keith Huff, he was my first potential intern in a new program I was to be a mentor in. That first potential intern made a great impression because I said "Yes," allowing him to become my first actual intern. The interview was Keith's first time to hear a film producer say, "YES," and would open the door to more new firsts. His first short film, first commercial, first music video, and many, many, more, but all as various crew roles, and not as the creative in charge.

Toward the end of his time working with me, Keith had to approach another new first, directing a short film. He wrote a phenomenally entertaining script and presented it to me. I flatly told him, "No." "You can't afford this," I said. "The set, the costumes, the CGI, you can't make this film. Not in the time we have or the budget. You need to try something else." His first time to hear a producer say, "NO!"

So, Keith dug deep and pulled from the depths of his imagination, *For Sale By Owner*. A simple, light-hearted comedy about a genuine problem we have all had to encounter, selling a vehicle. This screenplay would later become his "first" published short story. It was fun, grounded, sweet, charming, and most importantly, something we could accomplish—Keith's first Green-lit Film.

We then embarked on a journey through a whole series of new firsts, getting to the production of *For Sale By Owner*. First auditions, first hard decisions on casting a film from those auditions, ultimately led to Keith first time yelling, "ACTION" on a movie set of a short film he was directing.

There were many more firsts along the path to *For Sale By Owner*, becoming Keith's first finished film, first film festival entry, and first distributed film property, but they culminate in the volume you currently hold.

It has been my honor to walk with Keith, if only a short while on this bumpy road, working in the entertainment industry, and one thing I know for sure is that his talent and creativity will lead to many, many more firsts soon and for years to come. So happy reading, and please go watch, *For Sale By Owner* on amazon.com. Oh yeah, his first film on Amazon too!

Herschel Zahnd

May 4th, 2021

IV

INTRODUCTION

(Original)

Before my short story *For Sale By Owner* was the book you now hold, it was first a screenplay. It was written in the spring of 2015 and subsequently offered as my graduation project for The Film Connection. However, it was not the original script that I had developed while at film school. To complete my certificate, I was to direct the first ten minutes of the script I worked on with my screenplay mentor John Raffo (*Dragon: The Bruce Lee Story*, 1993, and *The Relic*, 1997). When it was time to submit the final product to my filmmaking mentor, Herschel Zahnd (*Girl Number Three*, 2009), it was turned down because production costs were too high.

For Sale By Owner became the second screenplay I ever wrote and was done so under extreme pressure. At the last minute, I was forced to write something brand new and have it ready to submit in less than a month. I remember being at work and goofing around with a friend (Josh). We started to make up scenes, not for a book or film but makeup stories for fun. It was on that day that the plot just hit me like lightning. *What if you had to sell a car, and you got the worst people ever to show up?* I knew I had the story I would develop for my film project with Herschel because it was simple yet profound. It did not seem like it would cost much to make. I was only supposed to write a ten-page screenplay with a beginning, middle, and end. When I was finished with the first draft, I had a problem. My script was over thirty pages long.

Herschel read the story and told me that I had to rework the script to meet the requirements. I remember him saying *the script is good, and I wish I could direct it.* I went back to alter the script and purposely took all the best scenes out. When Herschel read the second draft, he shook his head in disgust. He looked up at me and said, *Let's just make the whole thing!*

For Sale By Owner premiered on January 21st, 2018, on YouTube and later on Amazon.com. Later that year, Herschel submitted our film to a short film festival held at a local movie theater here in Louisville. I did not attend the showing because I had burned up all my sick days and personal days from making the movie. To this day, I regret not being there to see my film projected up on the silver screen in front of a live audience. Herschel attended and reported to me that our film received mixed reviews. Overall, the whole experience of filmmaking was great. I could not wait to start my next film project.

I finished film school in early 2016, and after that, I had no idea what to do next. Between 2016 and the film's release, I did get some work as a Production Assistant. I was lucky enough to P.A. one episode of *Master Chef* with Gordan Ramsay. Still, months passed with no work as a director. So, I decided to keep busy and turn my screenplay into my first short story. It was working on this project that I fell in love with writing.

Writing can be therapeutic, and crafting this story was a joy and a tribute to a difficult time in my life. My mother was recovering from chemotherapy. The threat was real that she might succumb to her illness before she could see me have any success. It is with high hopes that publishing this book and directing a movie will be enough to make her proud.

Keith Barnett Huff

June 15th, 2018

Louisville Kentucky

VIII

INTRODUCTION

(revised edition)

On July 15th, 2018, I released the first edition of *For Sale By Owner*. I did so with haste because my mother was unwell, and I wanted her to see and hold in her hands my first published book before she died. Unfortunately, in doing so, I released a book that was not professionally edited and contained within its pages many errors. After the book was published, I worked on two children's books and a book of poetry. I also took several writing classes at Harvard University. The results of my hard work expanded the scope of my writing skills. With a better understanding of writing, and editing I thought it was time to revisit *For Sale By Owner* and carefully examine it. I found those errors and decided the best action was to produce this revised edition.

In planning for the re-release of *For Sale By Owner*, I wanted to do something special. After re-editing the short story, I decided to expand on the material inside the book. I started by including more film set photos and this time have them be in full color. I am also pleased to incorporate in this new edition a foreword written by my film school mentor and executive producer Herschel Zahnd (*Girl Number Three*, 2009).

To this day, my short film *For Sale By Owner* is still as entertaining and profound as the day it was released. I am so very grateful to all those who helped me turn it into a reality. Creating this movie changed my life forever. It forced me to write. I initially did a lot of storytelling, but I could never get my ideas down on paper. With the proper motivation of a deadline and the chance to produce a film, this project was the push I needed to get me writing. And since then, I haven't stopped.

I would like to end this new introduction with the sad news that my mother died March 19th, 2019, from complications due to her battle with breast cancer. Although I had hoped she would see me have more success in life I am happy to report that she was very proud of me.

Keith Barnett Huff

June 15th, 2021

Louisville, Kentucky

FOR SALE
BY OWNER
(revised edition)

"The best thing a father can do for his children, is to love their mother."

-JOHN WOODEN

My father used to say, 'Family is the most important thing in the world. Second is the family vehicle. Because it always brought us together.' *I never understood what that meant. Not until the summer of 2015 when my mother and my father died. In the summer, I had to sell… the family van.*

A red cardinal follows the bend of the Ohio River between the neighboring cities of Louisville, Kentucky, and Jeffersonville, Indiana.

The Belle of Louisville, a white Mississippi-style steamboat with red paddles, drifts upriver. The vessel moves along at speed not fit for this era. Tourists on all decks enjoy the scene of Waterfront Park.

Adventure-seekers in colorful kayaks paddle past the exposed fossil beds of the Falls of the Ohio State Park. A rocky record of the Devonian period.

A barge hauling coal exits the Portland Canal, the only barrier to navigation between Pittsburgh and the Gulf of Mexico.

On this hot summer day, the good people of Kentuckiana are practically imprisoned by the heat inside their air-conditioned homes. A typical suburban neighborhood is nestled just beyond the city of Jeffersonville, Indiana.

On one cul-de-sac, a man dares the heat to cut his lawn.

On the opposite side of the street, a woman turns her water valve on then dashes back inside. A sprinkler comes to life, cascading water across a thirsty lawn.

The next house over, children splash, swim, and giggle in an above-ground pool. Their mother sunbathes on a lawn recliner. An old silver radio plays an upbeat tune and ends with a weather report from a smooth-talking host, "All right folks! Looks like another hot day with a high of 97 degrees!"

A man in red sunglasses bobs his head to the beats blasting into his ears from his red headphones. Walking his Jack Russell terrier around the bend of the sidewalk, his hound hangs its tongue, ready to return to the cold air of his master's home.

At the end of the cul-de-sac, a beat-up old tan van is parked in the driveway of a ranch-style house. A man, John, speaks exasperatedly on his cell phone as he places a For Sale By Owner sign inside the front windshield of the van. "I know, I know. I will sell it! A.S.A.P." John takes a deep breath. "Right now, I want to get rid of everything." He slams the door with frustration. He squints his eyes to watch at the end of his street heat waves dancing off the asphalt. Those ghostly waves remind him of an article he once read: Asphalt-melting heatwave kills over 1,100 people in India. He can't help but wonder if today's heat will liquefy this street.

"Have you seen the van yet?" she asks.

"I am looking at it right now. Can't we just keep the van?"

"Why? So, you can end up being the crazy guy who has an old rusted out vehicle forever parked beside his house."

"Like Uncle Henry?"

"Exactly!"

On the surface, John is a regular guy who is friendly and helpful. He had learned to be independent at an early age when his mother became sick.

John gives a light kick to the front tire. "Okay, fair point."

"Is it cleaned up and ready to sell?" she asks.

"Yes."

"Do you have any appointments?"

"I have three confirmed appointments coming," He licks his dry lips, "I was thinking to sell it for... two-thousand dollars."

"Are you kidding me? Sell it for two hundred.

A large white Chevrolet Camper Van with a rainbow streaming across its side turns onto his street.

"Sis, I got to go! I think my first appointment is here."

Wiping the sweat from his forehead, he returns the phone to his belt clip. *It's just an old van.* He thought.

Wearing a blue button-up shirt tucked into tan khakis, John quickly adjusts his black tie before patting his hair down.

The large white van rounds the cul-de-sac and parks sideways at the end of the driveway. The driver opens her door and leans out, looking at him over the van's roof. John sees a woman dressed in an array of purple and green with a burgundy headband. "Da darling, how are you?" She hops down and closes her door. As she rounds the front of her van, she lifts her hands to the sky. "What a glorious day this is! Our mother goddess shines down upon us." Her long fingers flutter to the sky.

"Ah… I'm good. You must be Maggie?"

"Darling, call me… Dreamcatcher," she says dreamily.

John notices that she is wearing dreamcatcher-themed jewelry that hangs around her ears and neck.

John extends his hand to welcome Dreamcatcher, but she moves past him in straight to the van.

"Yes, this is perfect! It's just what I was looking for!"

Rubbing his palms together, "Okay, great, you can take it for a test—"

Dreamcatcher whips her finger to John's lips. "Shh! I want to communicate with her first!"

John's hands fall to his sides, "Her?"

Dreamcatcher places her palms on the hood of the van. "Yes! I can feel her." She closes her eyes. "I can see her energy."

"Ahem. Great! Ah, well, I can tell you that this van has been taken great care of by my father."

With her eyes closed and head-turning side to side, Dreamcatcher senses something from the van. "She has a sad story. I will need to burn out the negative energy before I… take her apart."

John's eyes widen. "Take her apart!" he replies.

"Yes, darling. I like to sculpt, and I am looking for metal that has a powerful energy. I was drawn to this vehicle." Her hands ball up, shaking with excitement. "How much do you want for it?"

"I was thinking around ten thousand," John says, rubbing his neck.

"Ten thousand! Dollars?"

"Yes, ma'am."

"Kid, I'll give ya, seven hundred for it. Cash!"

"Nope, sorry. Ten thousand dollars."

"Look at this piece of crap! It is not even worth a couple of hundred bucks."

Mimicing her palm sensing gimmick, "Well, you know it… she is a special powerful soul."

"How about eight hundred bucks, ten free palm readings, and a custom-made dreamcatcher?" she offers, nodding with excitement.

John's mouth falls open.

John feels mocked as he watches a yellow smiley face tire cover blankly stare back at him as Dreamcatcher drives away.

"What a wacko!"

John's phone lights up with a picture of his sister, and the words "Joyce calling" appear.

"Hello?"

"How's the sale going?" Joyce asks.

"Uh?"

"You didn't sell it?"

"No."

"Okay?" she says, waiting for the excuse.

"I cannot force people to buy the van, Joyce. She didn't like it. So, relax. I still have more appointments coming." John walks up the driveway. Sweat is beading down his face.

"You want to come over for dinner?" she asks.

"No, I have plans tonight."

"Eating alone again?"

"I've got a ton of work to catch up on."

"John, you shouldn't be alone all the time."

"I'm not alone. Not while I have you checking up on me all the time."

"You know what I mean."

John opens his front door and is hit by a refreshing wave of cool air. Before he can step inside his home a deep voice yells out, "Hey, buddy! Is this the van for sale?"

John turns back to see at the end of the driveway a well-dressed man grinning from ear to ear. Standing next to him is his teen son. "Got to go!" John says, hanging up.

Game music and action sounds emanate from a smartphone in the teen's hands. The teen's eyes are zeroed in on the device.

Hands on his hips, the father examines the old, dented van.

John wears a fake smile and waits for the father to finish. "So, is this van for you or your son?"

"For my son!" the man says with a sour look on his face.

"Great! Are you excited about taking care of a vehicle?" John asks the son.

The teen ignores him as he keeps playing, not missing a beat. "Come on, die! Die! Die! Yes!"

"The man is asking you a question, son."

The boy looks up for only a moment. "What? Yeah, whatever."

The father laughs. "Kids today! Well, sport, let's take her for a spin."

John feels a big lump emerge in the back of his throat. He pauses a moment before he retrieves the keys from his pants pocket and hands them over to the father.

The father turns to his son and tosses the keys to him.

Distracted from playing his video game the keys hit his chest and the boy catches them as they fall. He pockets his phone and moves to the driver side of the van.

Opening the passenger side door, the father looks to John. "We'll be right back." He says with a big smile.

While sitting on his front porch, John drums on his phone, nervously waiting for the father and son's return.

Should I have gone? Checking the time on his phone, he sees that twenty minutes have now passed since they left to test drive the van. "Where the hell are they?"

The tan van speeds down a two-lane street until it violently turns into an empty school parking lot. The left front tire misses the road and hits a puddle, throwing water and mud into the air. The van turns and suddenly stops, throwing the driver and passenger forward then back.

The son takes a moment to enjoy the adrenaline pumping through his neck.

The father catches his breath. "God damn it! Take it easy, son. You don't want to mess up this guy's van any more than it already is."

The son rolls his eyes. "Sorry."

"Alright. Now back her up easy, son. Get us in that parking space nice and—"

The boy puts the van in reverse and hits the gas. The van kicks back, nearly jumping into the empty parking space. The son hits the breaks just in time.

The father lets out a long, soft whistle. "Okay. Not bad. Slower next time. Let's try parallel parking next. You're doing great, son," he says, placing a firm hand on his son's shoulder.

"Okay," the son replies blankly.

The father balls his fists and pounds it on the dash. "You know, the time will come when you're a parent, and you'll be dreaming of the day when you finally get to teach your son how to drive."

"Yeah, Dad, I am counting down the days."

The son drives the van back out to the main road not pausing before merging into oncoming traffic.

John stands as he sees his van turning to come back down his street. Red in the face, he straightens his tie and takes a deep breath to relieve some of his stress.

The van pulls into the driveway and stops with a sudden jerk.

Exiting the van, the son is back on his phone playing his game.

John is on his heels. "So, what do you think? Judging by how long you were gone, I would say you must be interested?"

Over his shoulder, the son tosses John the keys, closes the door, and walks back toward his father's black Mercedes Benz.

John plays hot potato with the keys as he tries to catch them from falling from his grasp. He stares back in disappointment.

Rounding the van, holding a water bottle heavy with condensation, the father shakes John's hand. The man's eyes are hidden by his dark aviator sunglasses. "Yeah, about that, we're going to pass. Thanks anyway."

"Something wrong?"

"No, we just want to pass," the father says, looking over the brim of his glasses.

"I can come down on the price!" John fires back.

"Thanks, but we want to keep looking."

John steps forward, trying to make one last push. "But—"

The man spins his car keys around his finger and smiles. "It's a fine vehicle, but my son wants something... a little more his style. You understand, right?" he says, patting John's shoulder before heading back to his car. "Sucker," he whispers out the side of his mouth.

John forces a smile. "Okay! Thanks for looking."

After the father and son leave, John kicks a rock off his driveway. Letting the van go from one family to another would have been perfect for clearing his conscience.

Walking past the van, he notices a mud smudge on the back-side window. He gently rubs it off with his sleeve. As he backs away from the van, a mysterious man wearing all black has appeared from nowhere. He stands to the side of John's yard, holding a black umbrella and wearing a black top hat. In a British accent, he asks, "Is the van for sale?"

John stumbles back and catches himself on the side of the van. He looks briefly at the goth man before his eyes dart around, trying to figure out where this mysterious apparition could have been hiding. "Umm... yes!"

John lifts open the rear door of the van. "As you can see, there is plenty of space."

The man pushes past John and crawls in to lay down on his back. His torso and head lay between the captain's chairs. Crossing his arms over his chest and closing his eyes the Goth man rest.

"What… what are you doing?"

The man in black cocks his head up. "Do ye think there is room for a coffin?"

"Get out!" John says through his teeth.

The goth man shrugs and slides himself forward out of the van.

John closes the hatch door. "How much crazier can this day get?"

A short time later…

John rests on the side door of the van that is opened for inspection. "I really don't think all of you will fit inside!"

Surrounding the van, fifty clowns practice their performance acts waiting on the response of their leader.

The head clown pops his body halfway out of the van's side entrance. "Can we at least try?" he asks, with a big red grin that reaches from ear to ear.

All around the van, the clowns squeeze their rubber clown horns.

Honk-a, honk-a! echoes across the cul-de-sac.

John blankly stares with his mouth open in disgust.

Shortly after that…

A Hollywood movie director rounds the backside of the van with his fingers to his thumbs, making a camera window. He is mapping out his shot of the vehicle. He is followed by his assistant, jotting down everything he says. The assistant has an arsenal of production gear, from his pocket-covered vest to his pocket-covered pants, including a megaphone tightly held under his arm.

"It is perfect!" the director yells, "we can use this in our end shot. We can crash it, burn it, then throw it off a cliff!"

The assistant continues writing frantically.

"I want Amy from Trans. Poe. to have it on set in twenty minutes!" He clenches his fists. "I want *bold*. I want *cinematic!*" He takes the megaphone from his assistant and fires it into his face. "*I! Want! Epic!*" Then storms off heading back to their production truck.

Shaking off the abuse, the assistant follows.

"A *cliff*?!" John yells back.

Four young Chinese college students argue in Mandarin at one another over the quality of the van. The first argues that the van is reasonable, but the second counters it will be bad for the environment.

A girl wearing high heels and a dress doesn't want to be seen in an old, beat-up van.

A fourth girl is wearing sweatpants and a t-shirt with the phrase, I Don't Care, stenciled upon it. Her eyes never leave her phone.

"Ladies?" John asks politely.

The girls continue to argue back and forth ignoring him.

"Uh… ladies?"

The four young Chinese girls escalate their argument this time pointing at one another.

With enough gust to cause an avalanche, John screams, "*Ladies!*"

The paddles of a bamboo wind chime drum a soft beat as a gentle wind blows in, cooling down the summer heat.

John, seated on the front porch, stares at the beat-up old van. He listens peacefully to the bamboo chime that hangs off the front porch of his parents' house. In a meditative state while drinking the last drops of water from his crumpling plastic bottle. He is drawn back to reality when his phone rings. *Anyone but my sister!*

His phone lights up with the name Joyce.

John lets out a deep sigh, stands, and presses the red answer button. "Hi, sis."

"And?" she asks.

"Not today!" he says, squinting his eyes.

"I told you. I should have sold the van. But, instead, I have to do everything!"

"Well, I look forward to seeing how easily you can sell the house."

"John, I just sold the house."

John's face goes pale. "What? You sold it?" He seeks shade in the shadow of the side of his childhood home. "That's great!"

"It's more than what we were asking. So, I told the buyers we could be out by the end of the month."

"End of the month? Sure. I can come by this weekend and pick up my stuff." John rests himself against the rough brick.

"Okay, well, the will says that we have to split up Mom and Dad's stuff ourselves."

"I don't want anything."

"No, you need to keep something of –"

"I'll take some family photos and some of moms' paintings," John says walking back to the front yard. He stops when he sees a thin young woman peering into the passenger side window of the van. "I need to go. Looks like I have one more."

"Sell the van—"

John hangs up.

The young lady sees John and a smile fills her face. Bursting with positive energy. She is wearing a grey, penguin-lovers-themed shirt with white shorts. Along with a very noble face, her overall look suggests that she has tremendous inner beauty.

"Hello," John says.

"Hi!" the young woman says pushing herself up on her tiptoes. "Is this the van for sale?"

"Yes. Yes, it is."

"Okay, great. I didn't see a sign."

"Yeah, uh, I must have forgotten to put it back."

"Your ad says two thousand?"

"Yes. That is the asking price. My name is John… Robertson." He says, reaching out to shake her hand.

"I'm Ariana… Holloway," she responds playfully, waving before accepting his hand.

John guides her over to the driver's door and opens it up for her.

A smile never seems to leave Ariana's face. As she sits behind the wheel, she surveys the quality of the van's interior. "Overall, I like it. What year is it?"

"Ah... two thousand."

"Like your asking price!"

"Yes," he says with a nervous laugh.

Ariana runs her fingers through her hair. "Well, mind if I take her for a test drive?"

"No! Not at all," he says, closing the door for her. He dashes to the passenger side. Inside, he buckles his seatbelt and drums his knees in excitement.

"Um, I need the keys."

"Oh! Right." Blushing, he struggles to find the keys. After digging them out of his pants pocket, he accidentally drops them between the seats.

They both bend over to retrieve them at the same time which causes them to bump heads.

"Sorry, are you okay?" Ariana asks.

"Yes, are you okay?"

"Yes, no worries."

He places the keys on Ariana's open palm.

Ariana starts up the van.

A warm blast hits them both before it slowly turns cool.

After being outside most of the afternoon, John takes a moment to enjoy the cold refreshing air. "It sure is hot today."

"Oh, it's been awful."

After making all the adjustments needed for her body size, she is ready to go. She is about to pull the gear from park to reverse but stops as she realizes she has forgotten something. She reaches into her purse between the seats. She picks and shovels until she finds her treasure—a small three-inch homemade clay penguin figure. She sticks it to the dashboard.

John stares at the clay penguin with curiosity.

"Sorry, I do not go anywhere without this little guy. He's for good luck! His name is Herman."

"Oh!" John says, loving this weird kind of cuteness.

"Okay! Let's roll." Ariana says, shifting the van into reverse.

The van pulls out of the neighborhood and continues down a twisting road toward the Ohio River.

John's attention is on the clay penguin with its painted eyes that stare back at him.

Looking at Ariana's shirt and then back to the waving Herman on the dashboard, John ponders about her apparent obsession with penguins. "So, do you like penguins?" he asks sarcastically.

"Ha! No, I love them!"

"I can see that. Why do you love penguins?"

"Oh, I don't know. You don't have a favorite animal or thing in your life that you obsess over?"

Playing with the air vents, John thinks for a moment. In his youth, he wanted to travel the world. One destination that appealed to him was Australia. The main reason was that it was home to his favorite childhood animal, the kangaroo. "Kangaroos! I remember liking kangaroos."

Ariana senses sadness in John's response. "Okay, why kangaroos?"

"Oh, ah." John thinks for a moment. "They're like giant rabbits with pockets. I thought it would be great to have a pocket to put stuff in."

"You know only the females have pockets, right?"

"Yeah, of course," John says with a chuckle. Then, looking out the side window, John says in a low voice, "I do now."

Ariana holds back a laugh. "I love penguins because they are cute and social, and the males help incubate the eggs."

"Okay, and what type of penguin is Herman?"

"Herman! Oh, he's a Gentoo penguin. They're my favorite. You know, penguins are also romantic," she says, raising an eyebrow at him.

"Ah... romantic?"

With an earnest tone, Ariana responds, "Yeah, penguins are just one of many species that stay together for life."

"Huh!"

"Yeah, the yellow-crested penguin will return to the place where they were born to meet a suitable partner. When a penguin's mate gets sick or dies, they mourn. Some even die because they stop grooming themselves." Then, her tone switches to hopeful. "It is sad, but... it's romantic. They love their companions."

"Ah!" he responded. His eyes locked with Herman's.

Turning on to River Road heading west, the van passes under the George Rogers Clark memorial bridge. A cantilevered truss bridge that connects downtown Jeffersonville to downtown Louisville.

The van continues down a windy road alongside Ashland Park and the Ohio River. On the opposite side of the waterway the Louisville skyline rises and falls.

White clouds appear, helping to cool down the region.

The van now passes under the Pennsylvania Railroad Bridge.

"So, is there anything wrong with the van I should know about?" Ariana asks.

"It does have a lot of miles, as you can see. Some minor body damage...." A memory suddenly strikes him. A moment long ago when his sister was learning to drive. Joyce was backing the van out of the garage, and she guided it too close to the side of the entrance, scratching paint off. "My father took great care of this—"

Bang!

The van vibrates violently as smoke pours from under the hood.

Ariana and John lock eyes a moment.

Johns face flushes.

Ariana drives the van off the main road and into a nearby parking lot of Ashland Park. "What happened?"

"I... I don't know. Pull in there," pointing toward an empty parking space looking straight out toward the river.

The van coasts into the space.

John opens his door and moves to the front of the van. "Pop open the hood."

Ariana switches on the emergency lights, turns off the engine, and unbuckles to get out. She quickly examines the area under the steering wheel until she finds the hood latch and pulls the release lever.

John opens the released hood.

A cloud of black smoke rolls out.

Ariana is by his side now. "Do you have roadside assistance?" she asks, using her hand as a visor to block the sun.

John quickly thumbs at his cell phone looking for a number. "I can call a tow truck. I'm so sorry. I'm so embarrassed. This is the worst time I have ever had selling anything." He finds what he needs and presses call. "I... I hope you don't think this is some kind of a scam."

"Oh, it's—"

"Yes, hello!" John says to the operator.

A glance at her watch tells Ariana she should rethink her day.

A colorful sign on the other side of the road catches her eye, that summons an innocent smile to her heart-shaped face. "Hey, I'll be right back."

"I need help immediately!" Distraught and without thinking, John walks in the opposite direction toward the river. "How long?" he shouts.

After ending his call, John collapses onto a green park bench. He stares out across the dark river water to the Kentucky side where he sees downtown Louisville. The towering skyline stretches from east to west. Afternoon sun light burnishes the glass, steel, and marble surfaces of the classical and modern structures. John gazes across the park watching children playing, then at a group of ducks waddling into the riverbank. They glide peacefully into the cool water. His attention now shifts to a barge full of coal that slowly enters the Portland Canal. None of these things seem to distract him from the sadness that he feels.

"Hope you like chocolate!" Ariana says handing him a bowl of melting chocolate ice cream.

John has completely forgotten that he is not alone. "Oh! Ah…thanks. I do, actually," John takes the bowl and straightens his posture, "I am… so sorry about the van," he says, holding back his emotion.

"What is it?" Ariana asks, sitting next to him.

John eats a spoon full of the sweet treat.

She joins in with her pink strawberry dessert.

"I don't know why the van just… died. My father took such great care of it." John loosens his tie. "Look, we are at least five miles away from my house. Let me call you a taxi or a—"

"No, it's okay."

"The woman on the phone said the tow truck won't be here for at least two hours."

"I am not going to abandon you here."

John stares into his bowl.

"The van is not yours, is it?" Ariana asks.

John shakes his head, avoiding eye contact. "It was my mother's until she died. Then my father took care of it until… he died."

"Aw… I am so sorry."

"Remember your penguin story?"

Ariana nods.

"It is kind of like that. You would not believe the day I'm having. I did not know it would be this hard letting go of everything."

"It's hard letting go of the things that remind us of the people we love."

It had been a long time since John could remember not wanting a day to end because of the presence of another.

"This is good ice cream," he says, nodding his head with approval.

Ariana smiles. "I love this place. My parents used to bring me here all the time when I was little... and sometimes now." She says, rolling her eyes in embarrassment.

John looks back to see the condition of the van. "Well, looks like the van stopped smoking."

Ariana confirms with a guilty smile.

"Somehow, I know this will be a stupid question, but have you been to the Louisville Zoo?"

"Yes! But not recently," she says, her eyebrows raised.

"If you are not doing anything this weekend, would you like to go to the zoo... with me?"

Ariana blushes. She pauses to swallow the cold dessert.

"We can see the penguins!" He looks back into his bowl and shakes his head.

Ariana fights the temptation to smile at his sudden boldness and immediate awkwardness. She looks toward the Ohio River to hide her smile. Then, after thinking for a few seconds, she happily responds. "Sure, and the kangaroos."

Looking into her eyes, he feels a surge of happiness.

Before taking another bite, Ariana asks, "I hope you have another vehicle. I do not drive on the first date."

"Don't worry. I have my own car."

At that moment, John remembers the quote his father used to say: *Family is the most important thing in the world. Second is the family vehicle. Because it always brought us together.*

THE END

You've Read The Book!

Now Watch The Film!

Renegade Art Productions Presents

A **Keith L. Huff** Film

Patrick Vaughn & **Chelsea Skalski**

FOR SALE BY OWNER

Featuring **Jayson William Allen**

Sound by **American Recording Company**

Executive Producer **Herschel Zahnd**

Written, Produced, and Directed by **Keith L. Huff**

Scan the Q.R. Code Below and Watch the Film Now for FREE on YouTube!

34

FOR SALE
BY OWNER

ORIGINAL SCRENNPLAY

by

KEITH BARNETT HUFF

© 2015

FOR SALE BY OWNER

Renegade Art Productions Presents
A **Keith Barnett Huff** Film
Patrick Vaughn & **Chelsea Skalski**
For Sale By Owner
Featuring **Jayson William Allen**
Sound by **American Recording Company**
Executive Producer **Herschel Zahnd**
Written, Produced, and Directed by **Keith Barnett Huff**

For My Wife,
Guo Yuanyuan

"FOR SALE BY OWNER"

Black screen.

Insert quote:

> "The best thing a father can do for his
> children, is to love their mother."
>
> -John Wooden

Fade in:

SCENE 1

EXT. SUBURBAN INDIANA - LATE MORING

*A row of houses line around a cul-de-sac street.
It's a typical suburban neighborhood. The
Sounds of a lawn mower powering up, followed
by a dog bark.*

CUT TO:

CLOSE ON TALL GRASS mowed down by a lawnmower.

CUT TO:

CLOSE UP SPRINKLER, watering a front lawn.

CUT TO:

A MAN, dressed for summer, walking his dog on the sidewalk.

CUT TO:

PUSH IN to an old beat-up tan colored VAN.

> JOHN (*v.o.*)
>
> My father once told me; Family is the most important thing in the world. The family vehicle is second because it is what always brought us together.

A FOR SALE BY OWNER sign, is placed in the front windshield of the VAN by a MAN in his

late twenties. He is talking on his smart phone.
After he closes the front passenger door he
circles back behind the van. This is JOHN; he
is wearing khaki dress pants and a blues blue
dress shirt with a black tie.

                    JOHN
          (*wipes sweat from his forehead*)
     I know, I know. I will do it A.S.A.P! Right
     now, I need to get rid of everything. Yeah.
     Ahem. I am looking at right now.

John moves the front driver's side. He lightly
kicks the front driver side tire.

                    JOHN
     I have three confirmed appointments
     coming today. I think I can sell it for... two
     hundred dollars.

A large white VAN with a yellow roof and a
rainbow of colors streaming down its side,
turns down his street.

JOHN

(*aware of the approaching van*)

I need to go, sis, I think my first appointment is here. I can sale it! I'm going to sale it. I need to go, bye!

The HIPPIE looking van parks in front of John's driveway. A WOMAN steps out from the vehicle. This is DREAMCATCHER and she is wearing an all gypsy-esk attire.

DREAMCATCHER

(*hands flutter to the sky*)

Da darling, how are you? What a glorious day this is. Our mother goddess shines down upon us.

JOHN

(*extends his hand*)

Ah, I'm good. Are you Maggie?

DREAMCATCHER

(*moving past him*)

Darling, call me... Dreamcatcher. Yes, this is perfect! It's just what I was looking for.

Dreamcatcher hovers her palms over the hood of the van.

JOHN

(*confused*)

Okay, great you can take it for a—

DREAMCATCHER

(*places her finger to his lips*)

Shh! I'm communicating with her.

JOHN

(*surprised*)

Her?

DREAMCATCHER

Yes! I can feel her. I can see her energy!

                    JOHN

Ahem. Great, I can tell you that this car has
been taken great care of—

                DREAMCATCHER

(*sadden*)

She has a sad story, a tragic story. I will
need to burn out the negative energy before
I... take her apart.

                    JOHN

(*hysteric*)

Take her apart!

                DREAMCATCHER

(*casual*)

Yes, darling. I like to sculpt, and I'm looking
for metal that has powerful energy. I was
drawn to this vehicle. How much do you
want?

                    JOHN

(*rubbing his neck with a look of disgust*)

I was thinking... ten thousand.

DREAMCATCHER

(*steps backward*)

Dollars!

John nods in response.

DREAMCATCHER

(*dropping her act*)

Look, kid, I'll give you five hundred bucks
for it. Cash!

JOHN

Nope. Sorry. Ten thousand.

DREAMCATCHER

(*hands on her hips*)

Look at this piece of crap. It's not even
worth a thousand!

JOHN

(*hovering his palms above the hood*)

Well, you know she is a special... powerful
soul!

DREAMCATCHER

(*stepping uncomfortable close to John*)

How about seven hundred bucks! Ten free
palm-readings! And... a custom-made
dreamcatcher!

CLOSE UP of John's disappointed face.

CUT TO:

*A yellow winking happy face tire cover stares
at John as Dreamcatcher's colorful van speeds
off down his street.*

JOHN

(*concerned*)

What a wacko!

John's phone rings.

JOHN

(*walking to his front porch*)

Hello? No Joyce, I did not. I will. I will. I still have two more. I have plans tonight. I'm eating at home. I appreciate it.

John reaches to open his front door.

UNKNOWN MALE

(*yelling*)

Hey buddy!

CUT TO:

Standing at the end of his driveway is a middle-aged MAN and a young TEEN.

MAN

(*shouting*)

Can we look at the van?

SCENE 2

EXT. DRIVEWAY - LATE MORNING

The FATHER examines the van, while his SON plays an extremely violent VIDEO GAME.

John wears a fake smile while he waits as the Father finishes examining the exterior of the van.

                    JOHN
(*nervous*)
So, this vehicle for you or your son?

                    FATHER
(*annoyed*)
It's for my son.

                    JOHN
(*fake enthusiasm*)
Great! Are you excited about taking care of
a van?

                    SON

(*shrugs*)
Whatever.

The Father shakes his head in disappointment.

                    SON

(*screams at his smartphone*)
Come on, die! Die! Die! Yes!

                  FATHER

(*laughing*)
Kids today.

                   JOHN

(*clearing his throat*)
Right.

                  FATHER

(*holds out his hand for the keys*)
Well, let's take it for a spin!

John hesitates a moment.
The Father snatches the KEYS away.

CUT TO:

*John sitting on his front porch waiting
impatiently.*

Checking the time on his smart phone.

*Twenty minutes have passed since the Father
and Son left.*

                    JOHN
Where the hell are, they?

SCENE 3

EXT. SCHOOL PARKING LOT - LATE MORNING

*The tan van speeds down a side street. It
suddenly turns hard into a SCHOOL parking
lot. The front tire misses' part of the road and
splashes into a muddy puddle.*

Muddy water splashes high into the air.

*The van turns sharply into the center of the
empty school parking lot. Then stops violently.*

INSIDE OF THE VAN

*The father is thrown forward than backwards
into his seat.*

                    FATHER
          (*shaking his head*)
     Okay! Now back up into the parking space.

The van jumps back into the space and stops
with such force the Father is nearly thrown
from his seat.

                    FATHER
(*holding on tight*)
God damn it, son! Take it easy! You do not
want to mess up this guy's van anymore
than it already is.

                     SON
Whatever.

                    FATHER
(*mentoring*)
Okay! Now let's work on your parallel
parking. You're doing great son.

The Father places a supporting hand on his
son's shoulder.

                     SON
Whatever!

FATHER

(*disgusted*)

You know when you become a parent, you will dream of the day when you can teach your son how to drive.

SON

(*fake enthusiasm*)

Great!

The Son puts the van into drive.

CUT TO:

WIDE VIEW OF THE PARKING LOT:

The van bolts forward and speeds to the exit, then stops violently. After another car passes the van speeds out onto the road with a hard-screeching turn.

SCENE 4

EXT. JOHNS DRIVEWAY – DAY

The van finally returns.

John is angry and ready to hit someone. Sitting up he calmly pushes down his anger.

The van pulls into the driveway. As the engine shuts off, the Father and Son exit.

John shifts his personality into salesperson mode.

> JOHN
>
> So, what do you think? Judging by how long you were gone I'd say you must be interested.

> FATHER
> (*sunglasses on*)
> I think we're going to pass.

Before walking back to his car, the Son tosses the keys blindly toward John.

JOHN

(*catching the keys in his chest*)

Something wrong?

FATHER

No, no. we're just going to pass.

JOHN

(*desperate*)

I can come down on the price! If you are
interested.

FATHER

(*spins his keys*)

It's a fine vehicle. My son wants something
a little more... his style. Thanks anyway.

JOHN

(*disappointed*)

Okay, thanks for looking.

FATHER

(*soft voice walking away*)

Sucker!

The Father and Son climb into a black
Mercedes Benz.

John waves goodbye. As soon as the black car
disappears so does his smile.

> JOHN
> (*spinning around in anger*)
> Damn it!

SCENE 5

EXT. JOHNS DRIVEWAY – DAY

*John looks over the van. Nothing seems to be
wrong except a mud smudge on the back-side
window. He wipes the smudge off.*

*Stepping away, a MAN dressed in all black
goth attire holding an umbrella is waiting
behind him.*

GOTH MAN
(*British accent*)
Is the van for sale?

JOHN
(*caught off guard*)
Wow! Where did you come from?

GOTH MAN
(*tipping his black top hat*)
The van, is it for sale?

INSIDE THE VAN

The GOTH MAN is laying down eyes closed with his arms crossed in a R.I.P. gesture. John is resting, annoyed, against the back-hatch door.

                    GOTH MAN
         (*head up, eyes open*)
         Is there room for a coffin?

                    JOHN
         (*soft angry tone*)
         Out!

CUT TO:

A moment later. John closes the back hatch door with great force.

                    JOHN
         How much crazier can this day get?

SCENE 6

EXT. JOHN'S DRIVEWAY – DAY

CLOSE UP of John standing next to the open side door of the van.

> JOHN
>
> (*disgusted*)
>
> I really don't think you are all going to fit inside!

Honk-a! Honk-a!

A CLOWN pops out of the side of the van.

> LEAD CLOWN
>
> (*smiling with wonder*)
>
> Can't we at least try?

WIDE SHOT of the street; fifty or more CLOWNS surround the van.

SCENE 7

EXT. JOHN'S DRIVEWAY - DAY

A movie DIRECTOR and his young ASSISTANT move quickly around the van. The Director is using both his hands and fingers to create a window to plot out his shot.

His Assistant writes frantically everything he says.

                    DIRECTOR
This is perfect! Just what we need. I can
use this in the final shot. I'm going to crash
it! Burn it! Then... throw it off a cliff! Call
Amy from transit; I want her here *A.S.A.P!*

The Assistant continues to scribe.

                    DIRECTOR
(*serious tone*)
I want bold! I want daring!

DIRECTOR

(holding the megaphone to his assistant's face)

I! WANT! EPIC!

The Director storms off.

The Assistant shake off the abuse and follows.

JOHN

(*to the Director*)

A CLIFF!

SCENE 8

EXT. JOHN'S DRIVEWAY – DAY

Four CHINESE college girls argue in Mandarin.

John watches quietly off to the side as he is not sure how to handle the four young women.

JOHN

(*calmly*)

Ah, ladies!

SUNFLOWER GIRL

(*in Chinese Mandarin*)

This is the most practical for the amount we have.

HIPSTER GIRL

(*in Chinese*)

This van is not good for the environment!

JOHN

(*starting to lose his cool*)

Ah, ladies, please.

POSH GIRL

(*in Chinese*)

OMG, I'm not going to be seen riding around in this piece of junk!

SLOB GIRL

(*in Chinese*)

I'm hungry.

John loses his patients.

JOHN

(*yelling up to the sky*)

LADIES!

SCENE 9

INT. JOHN'S FRONT PORCH – DAY

A soft wind blows the paddles of a bamboo wind chime. Sitting on the steps of his front porch, John loosens his tie and unbuttons his top shirt collar. He stares at the van with the feeling of defeat.

His phone rings.

John looks at the screen to see who's calling. JOYCE. John releases a breath of air as he answers the call.

                    JOHN
        (*walking to the side of his house*)
Hi sis. No, they did not like it. This is not like last time. I'm not picky. I want to sell it! I promise. Look the first lady was crazy. The second person was a father looking for a car to buy his son. The third? Well.... You know, they were not interested. And there

were more but. I can sell it. What? You
already sold the house?

John walks back to the front of the house.

JOHN

That is... great. Good for you. I can come by
this weekend to pick up my stuff. I don't
want anything of Mom and Dad's. Joyce, I
just want to keep some photos and maybe
some of mom's paintings.

*A WOMAN is now looking into the side window
of the van.*

JOHN
(*now aware of the woman*)

Ah... I need to go!

SCENE 10

EXT. FRONT OF THE HOUSE – DAY

The WOMAN is ARIANA she is in her late twenties, wearing a grey t-shirt with a penguin couple holding hands.

                    JOHN
        (*nervous*)
        Hello!

                    ARIANA
        (*holding out an ad*)
        Yes! I was wondering if you could tell me
        about the vehicle. I see you want two
        thousand for it is that correct?

                    JOHN
        Yes. Yup. That's what I'm asking for it. I'm
        John... Robertson.

                    ARIANA
        (*playfully*)
        I'm Ariana... Holloway.

John and Ariana shake hands.

JOHN

Let's have a look, shall we?

INT. VAN – DAY

Ariana is seated behind the steering wheel.
She checks out all the compartments and looks
over all the buttons on the dash.

John is waiting just outside the driver side
door.

ARIANA

Overall, I like it. What year is it?

JOHN

Ah... two thousand.

ARIANA

(*smiling*)

Like your asking price.

                              JOHN
              (*smiling back*)
              Yes.

                             ARIANA
              (*running her fingers through her hair*)
              Okay! Mind if I take it for a test drive?

                              JOHN
              (*closing the door*)
              Absolutely!

OUTSIDE THE VAN

*John hurries around the vehicle. He pats down
his wet hair.*

INSIDE THE VAN

*John climbs into the passenger seat. After he
buckles in his seatbelt, he taps his knees.*

*ARIANA stares at him. She is waiting for him
to give her the keys.*

                    ARIANA
(*light laugh*)
Ah... I need the keys.

                     JOHN
(*social laugh at his own mistake*)
Oh! Right.

*Digging into his pants pocket, he finds them
only to drop them between their seats. Both
reach down to pick them up but then bump
heads.*

                     JOHN
(*embarrassed*)
Sorry!

                    ARIANA
(*rubbing her head*)
It's okay.

*John places the keys on Ariana's' palm. There
is a pause and a moment between the two.*

Ariana powers up the van. Warm air blast them both. After a moment the air turns cool. Ariana adjusts the vehicle to her needs. She goes to put the van in reverse. But pauses and she suddenly remembers something. She then retrieves a small, handmade, clay PENGUIN from her purse and places it on the dashboard.

CLOSE UP ON THE CLAY PENGUIN.

> ARIANA
> (*embarrassed*)
> Sorry, I don't go anywhere without this little guy. His name is Herman. I made him myself. He's for good luck!

John eyes the curious PENGUIN. It's childish and yet adorable.

> ARIANA
> (*putting the van in reverse*)
> Okay, let's roll!

EXT. NEIGHBORHOOD – DAY

*Ariana backs the van smoothly out of the
driveway.*

CUT TO:

*The van moves down a main road passing
restaurants. Out the driver's side window is
the OHIO RIVER.*
*Across the river is the skyline of downtown
LOUISVILLE KENTUCKY.*

SCENE 11

INT. VAN – DAY

John ponders about Ariana's penguin obsession.

                    JOHN
          (*nervous*)
          So, I was wondering. Do you like penguins?

                    ARIANA
          (*with great enthusiasm*)
          Ha! No. I love them!

                    JOHN
          (*a light laugh*)
          I can see that. So, why do you like
          penguins?

                    ARIANA
          (*thinks about the question*)
          I don't know. They speak to me.

JOHN

They speak to you?

ARIANA

Not literally. I mean I'm drawn to them.
Don't you have a favorite animal or thing in
your life you obsess over?

JOHN

Ah, kangaroos! I used to like kangaroos.

ARIANA

Okay, why kangaroos?

JOHN

Well, there like giant rabbits with pockets. I
thought it would be cool to have a pocket.

ARIANA

You know only the females have pockets.

                         JOHN
        (*soft voice*)
        Yeah! I do now.

                        ARIANA
        (*smiling*)
        I guess I love penguins because they're
        cute, there social, and the males incubate
        the eggs. They are also the most romantic
        animal.

                         JOHN
        Ah, romantic?

                        ARIANA
        Uh, yeah. When a penguin's mate dies the
        other will become depressed, they actually
        mourn. It's sad but romantic.

Ariana's story hits John on a personal level.

EXT. MAIN ROAD – DAY

The van drives under the GEORGE ROGERS CLARK MEMORIAL BRIDGE. They are nearing the FALLS OF THE OHIO STATE PARK.

INT. VAN – DAY

Following a long silence, Ariana brings the conversation back to the vehicle.

> ARIANA
> (*focused*)
> The van drives great. Is there anything else wrong with it?

> JOHN
> (*his mind elsewhere*)
> As you can see it has a lot of miles, some body damage. My father took great care of this—

BANG!
The van begins to shake.

ARIANA
(*startled*)
Wow! What was that?

JOHN
(*equally startled*)
I'm not sure! Pull over there.

Smoke begins to rise out from under the hood.

Ariana steers the van to an open space located at ASHLAND PARK.

SCENE 12

EXT. ASHLAND PARK - DAY

Hand over his mouth, John steps out and moves to the front of the van.

                    JOHN
     (*shouting to Ariana inside the van*)
     Pop the hood!

CUT TO:

Ariana's fingers moving down the side panel to find the hood latch. Once she finds it, she pulls up on the lever to release the hood.

CUT TO:

John raising the hood.

A cloud of black smoke rolls out.

Ariana joins John by his side.

ARIANA

(*sympathetic*)

Do you have roadside service?

JOHN

(*dialing his cell*)

I can... call a tow truck. I'm so sorry. I'm so
embarrassed. This is the worst time I've
ever had selling anything. I hope you don't
think this is some kind of scam.

ARIANA

I—

*Before she can answer, John is on his phone
walking towards the river.*

JOHN

Hello, I need help my van has broken down.

*Ariana checks her watch. She watches John a
moment. She turns and strides past the van.
Looking around she sees something of interest
across the street.*

ARIANA

(*calling out to John*)

Hey, I'll be right back.

JOHN

(*not listening*)

How long!

John sits slumped on a park bench with his phone holding up to his chin. He does not hide his depression. His gaze is fixed on the park.

The park is alive with kids running and jumping on a playground. Couples walk hand in hand. A few joggers move quickly across the scene. Teens on bikes race by. Ducks from the river waddle up the shore. Across the river, the skyline of Louisville rises and falls.

John slumps back into the bench.

ARIANA

(*passing John a bowl of ice cream*)

Hope you like chocolate!

JOHN

(*sitting up straight*)

I do, thanks! You didn't have to do this.

ARIANA

(*sitting next to him*)

Awe, it's okay.

JOHN

(*embarrassed*)

I don't know why the van just died. My father took such good care of it. After my mother died, he... I'm sorry, let me walk you back to your car. We're only a couple of miles away.

ARIANA

No, it's okay. I'm not going to abandon you here. So, your mother died. Is that why you're selling the van, for your father.

JOHN

My father died too. You see my mother died
battling cancer. After her death, he just
shut down. Kind of like your penguin story.

ARIANA

(*sympathizing*)

I'm sorry. If you want to talk about it—

JOHN

No, it's okay. I appreciate it. You just would
not believe the day I'm having. Today I
thought I was ready to sell my parents van
but...

ARIANA

Well, it's hard to let go of the things that
remind us of the people we love. It's
natural.

JOHN

(*reflecting*)

Mmm... This is good ice cream.

ARIANA

(*licking her spoon*)

I love this park. My parents use to bring me here all the time as a kid. This is our special place.

CUT TO:

WIDE SHOT OF WHOLE PARK SCENE. John and Ariana enjoying their ice cream.

CUT TO:

Looking out across the river JOHN draws in the beauty of the view across the river.

JOHN

Thanks for the ice cream, and thanks for waiting here with me.

ARIANA

(*chipper tone*)

It's fine!

JOHN

(*nervous*)

Hey, would you like to go to the zoo
sometime? We can see the penguins.

*John immediately regrets asking the question
fearing her rejection.*

ARIANA

(*smiling*)

Sure, and the kangaroos!

Insert song:
"Forever, Now and Then, For Sure"
by ARI MAC.

*John's eyes meet Ariana's. They can't help but
to smile.*

CUT TO:

WIDE SHOT OF THE PARK.

CAMERA moves from the side of the van, up toward the sky.

John and Ariana continue to talk and eat on the bench that sits at the beginning of a path that leads out of frame.

Downtown Louisville and the rest of the park are now in full view.

Insert voice narration of John.

My father once told me; Family is the most important thing in the world. The family vehicle is second because it is what always brought us together.

Cut to black.
Song continues over end credits.
End.

CAST & CREW

RENEGADE ART PRODUCTIONS Presents

A Keith L. Huff Film

For Sale By Owner

Directed by ....Keith L. Huff

Written by...Keith L. Huff

Produced by............................. Herschel Zahnd,

& Keith L. Huff

Director

of Photograph............................Herschel Zahnd

Editor...Herschel Zahnd

Costume Designer............................Keith L. Huff

Featuring Original Song By

Ari Mac, "Forever, Now and Then, For Sure."
From her album, *Soul Intact*.

-STARING-

Patrick Vaughn ....John Robertson

Chelsea Skalski..........................Ariana Holloway

Shelly Marquart Reid...................Dreamcatcher

Jeff McQueen..Father

Myles McClure...Son

-With-

Teresa Argote............................Creepy Buyer #4

Jonas J. Bangasser...................Creepy Buyer #3

Kellie Coleman...Drug Girl

Desiree Dean............................Creepy Buyer #2

Cory Elliot..Sk8ter Dude

Damon Gooch...Clown #3

Alphaeus Green Jr.............................Lead Clown

Dennis Grinar...Clown #2

Grace Guo....................................Chinese Girl #1

Keith L. Huff.......................Director's Assistant

Zhen Jia..Chinese Girl #4

Spencer Korcz.......................................Clown #1

Tiffany Ming Lin...........................Chinese Girl #3

Alexis Lusco...Convict

Jamer Mack..............................Creepy Buyer #1

Tina Wang Matzner.....................Chinese Girl #2

Peter Robertson............................Crazed Doctor

Chelsea Wolf..Clown #4

Herschel Zahnd....................Hollywood Director

-And-

Jayson Allen...Goth Man

FILM TERMS

Angle on – When the camera is focused upon either an object or a person.

Back to – The camera goes to an object or person, after moving from another.

Close on – From a close range the camera follows an object or person.

Cut to – Jumps to another scene.

Dissolve – The fading of a scene that is replaced with a new one.

EXT. – Exterior.

INT. – Interior.

Off-screen – Action or dialogue that happens off scree.

Pan – The camera moving from one point to another in a slow movement.

POV – Point of view.

Sotto voice – spoken as a whisper.

Voice over – Dialogue spoken over a scene, sometimes by characters not in the scene.

Set Photos:

FOR SALE BY OWNER

Filming John & Dreamcatcher

Director's Keith and Herschel in costume

Chelsea Skalski (Ariana) and Patrick Vaughn (John)

Widows Walk, Jeffersonville Indiana

Chelsea Skalski (Ariana) and Patrick Vaughn (John), keeping cool from the harsh heat.

Executive Producer & Cinematographer Herschel Zahnd

Graphics Designer Christopher Shiner

Shelly Marquart Reid (Dreamcatcher) & Director Keith Huff

Jeff McQueen (Father) and Myles McClure (Son)

Alphaeus Green Jr., Spencer Korcz, Chelsea Wolf,
& Dennis Grinar as the Clowns

Tina Wang Matzner, Tiffany Ming Lin,
Yuanyuan Grace Guo, & Zhen Jia as the Chinese Girls

Herman the Penguin
Sculpture by Joshua Schiller

The Robertson Family Van

APPENDIX I:

SYMBOLISM OF THE STORY

Symbolism is defined by Merriam-Webster as the art or practice of using symbols especially by investing things with a symbolic meaning or by expressing the invisible or intangible by means of visible or sensuous represen-tations. Simply put, symbolism is a language that can be used all around the world to understand the profound hidden meaning behind everything around us. From colors to numbers. From animals to plants. Everything has its own hidden meaning.

Carl Jung wrote: "Every psychological expression is a symbol if we assume that it states or signifies something more and other than itself which eludes our present knowledge." Jung believed that a collective unconscious connected all of humanity. This collective is a warehouse full of knowledge that all humanity taps into to draw from and add to.

Why use symbolism in stories? Authors and even filmmakers like to use symbolism in their work because it manages to help the reader better understand the concepts and follow the central themes. Artist use symbolism in their work to help fulfill the following:

- Adds emotional weight to the text.
- Help to relate large ideas in an organized and artistic way.
- Promote independent thinking among readers as they work through the interpreting of the author's work.

I wrote this article because I am fascinated by symbolism. Below is a breakdown of all symbols used in both the film and the short story.

John is the main character in the story, and he is going through a dark time in his life. There is an extreme need to reflect on his pain. For his clothing, he wears a bright blue dress shirt and black tie. Bright blue represents reflection. His black-tie expresses his grief, like a black armband of mourning.

Dreamcatcher or Maggie is a gypsy and claims to be a psychic. In a way, she is correct about her analysis of the van. Maggie wears dreamcatcher-themed neckless and earrings. With its circular shape, the dreamcatcher represents life's cycle, where death is part of the journey. Maggie is the first potential buyer of the van, and her role signifies the period that John's parents have traveled.

Father and Son represent the passing of the torch. However, in this story, it is all about subtext. The father is shady, and the son is distant and withdrawn. Their relationship is about lousy parenting. The father wants to have a father and son moment, and the son does not care. Parents shape their children to whom they will become.

Goth Man represents death, an invisible force that comes for us all. He also describes the death tarot card, which symbolizes transition—for example, the end of one thing and the next.

Clowns, according to a psychologist, are part of the hero myth. They represent a pinpoint for the first stage in the growth of a hero. The clowns are introduced after the Goth man as a symbol of John's moving forward.

Director and Assistant, in this story, represent man's obsession with destruction and abuse of power.

Chinese Girls represent aspects of humanity. If you study the scene carefully, how each girl is dressed, you can understand their personalities. One is dressed modestly in bright clothes. The second is an environmentalist with an orange headband and Earth tone color clothing. The third is vanity dressed, ready to go to a nightclub. The fourth is sloth and dressed as if she had just woken up. Their dialogue, although spoken in Mandarin Chinese, also fits with each personality. The vain girl refuses to be seen in an ugly van. The environmentalist is worried about the pollution the old van will emanate. The modest girl is excited about the vehicle's low cost, and the cell phone-addicted sloth is just concerned when they will eat.

Ariana wears a penguin-themed shirt and uses a penguin-themed charm named Herman. Penguins represent strong bonds that are loving and caring by nature.

The name Ariana means "Holy One," which are spiritual mentors. The final journey that John's traverses is his relationship with Ariana.

APPENDIX II:

HOW IT CAME TO BE:

The Origin of *FOR SALE BY OWNER*

"**O**ne person's craziness is another person's reality."

-Tim Burton

The screenplay of *For Sale By Owner* was written in March 2015, and the short film went into production in June of the same year. What many do not know is that the movie was never meant to be made. While I was attending film school, I had two projects to complete to graduate from the program. The first was writing a script that I would take with me to Los Angles and pitch to a real Hollywood producer. Second, I needed to direct one scene from that script with a runtime of five to ten minutes long. I was primarily choosing the best scene from that script to shot. There was one major problem. The cheapest scene would have cost somewhere in the ballpark of a million dollars to film.

To solve this problem Herschel Zahnd, my mentor at the time, assigned me to write a second script of five to ten pages long. That's a minute of screen time per page. It did not have to tell a whole story it just needed to be single scene. I was not thrilled about directing a scene. I wanted to direct a feature. My hands were tied I had no choice.

The idea of *For Sale By Owner* came to me while I was at work playing around with some goofy scenes with my friend and fellow artist, Josh Schiller. I joked about different types of crazy people trying to buy a guy's car and how their diverse personalities would create these funny scenarios. It was like getting struck by lightning. The idea just grew and grew, and I suddenly knew how the story needed to evolve. As soon as I got home from work, I began writing the script.

I completed my first draft of the screenplay with one problem. It was twenty pages over the limit. I thought, the hell with it, I'll let Herschel read it, and he can tell me what he thinks before I choose my scene to direct.

Herschel told me that my script was excellent, so good, in fact that he wanted to direct it himself. I remember him being really impressed with the story's simplicity, yet it had a complex emotional plot. The best part was how filmable it was. The production cost would be low, and the strength would come from the actor's performance. In the end, Hershel agreed to film the whole script. However, I would need to cut down to fifteen pages as he was not looking to go into a big project.

I cut the best scenes out, watered down the emotion, and took out all the in-house settings—this way, John's character is trapped outside. I built in this theme of John longing to go inside his house to get water and cool off, but another potential buyer would always show up, keeping him out in the heat.

After Herschel read the water-downed script, he realized that the story needed those great scenes and, without hesitation, immediately agreed to just make the film twenty minutes long. We both agreed the in-house scenes could go.

It was an exciting adventure directing my first short film. Once that was filled with extreme heat, thunderstorms, crew no-shows, and quick recast. You know, typical production woes. Filming was difficult in many ways. I could not truly focus my attention on being a director. There were many scenes that I directed while also holding a boom mic. It's hard to judge whether I've got the scene I imagined while I'm also trying to hold up a reflective photo screen so that the camera can pick up my actors. There was little to no time to re-watch scenes to know if what we got was any good. We had to go by instinct. Honesty, it's a miracle the film turned out as good as it is. I know there are flaws here and there. But you must know that this film was made with no money and since its release has generated no income. It was truly a labor of love.

The worst part of the whole experience was not being able to see my film on the big screen. We entered it into a local film contest that showed the film on the big screen. I had to work that night, so I missed it. To this day it is one of the biggest regrets in my life.

Most of the movie was filmed in Jeffersonville, Indiana. It would have been nice to film in my home state, but it turns out you must have permits to film in Kentucky. There is, however, a fantastic shot of the Louisville skyline at the end that makes up for it. That shot is my shout-out to my incredible city.

In the end, I would say that my time at the Film Connection was worth it. Not only did I get to direct a short film, but I also got to work with the local musician Ari Mac. She graciously let me use her van and her song, *Forever, Now and Then, For Sure*, for my end title song. I earned a certificate in Filmmaking and Screenplay writing. I got to go to Hollywood and pitch my screenplay, *Two Steps From Hell* to two Hollywood producers. While there, I go to walk around an actual television studio set. I made a lot of great memories working with everyone at Renegade Art Productions & American Recording Studio. I hope one day to work with Herschel. I think of him often and wish him the best.

One of the most important aspects of my journey was that it got me writing. Today I have published two children's books, a book of poetry, and several short stories. I don't know if I will ever direct again. But one thing I know for sure is that I will never stop telling stories.

APPENDIX III

Sources of Photographs

Huff, Keith. (2015). *For Sale By Owner.* Set
        photographs. Louisville, KY: NEXT PAGE
        PUBLISHERS LLC. Originally photographed in
        2015 & 2018.

Schiller, Joshua. (2015). *Sculpture of Herman.*
        Jeffersonville, IN: FISH WOOD INN

BIBLIOGRAPHY

Bruce-Mitford, M. (2004). *The illustrated book of signs & symbols*. New York: Barnes & Noble Books.

Ross, Elisabeth Kubler & Kessler, David. *Five Stages of Grief* (n.d.). Retrieved from https://grief.com/the-five-stages-of-grief/

Singh, H. S. (2015, May 28). Heatwave kills more than 1,100 in India. Retrieved April 26, 2018, from https://www.cnn.com/2015/05/25/asia/india-heatwave-deaths/index.html

Vogler, C., & Montez, M. (2007). *The writer's journey: Mythic structure for writers* (3rd ed.). Studio City, Ca.: Michael Wiese Productions.

ACKNOWLEDGMENTS

I would like to thank Renegade Art Productions for turning my screenplay into a short film. This project allowed me to work with the most talented people in Louisville. To all the artists who helped me achieve my dream of making *For Sale by Owner* a reality, I thank you. The following people I would like to thank personally for their contributions to the film.

Herschel Zahnd, my mentor, and the executive producer, who helped me to learn my craft of film directing. Herschel is an actor, writer, and director known for *Girl Number Three* and *The Trimmer*. Herschel runs his own production company Renegade Art Productions.

American Recording Company Engineer, mixer, and producer Jon Mattingly. Thanks to John who worked to capture and edit the sound for the film.

Ari Mac, who allowed me to use her song *Forever, Now and Then, For Sure,* from her album *Soul Intact*, in my film.

Also, her awesome van. Ari has produced two albums, *Soul Intact* and *A Singer, a Six-String, and a Song*, with a third on the way.

Patrick Vaughn who performed the character of John with such precise, intense emotion needed for the role. This was the most crucial casting of all, and Patrick did not disappoint. I knew within the first minute of meeting him that he was John.

Patrick has acted with such groups as Commonweal Theater Company, Actors Theater of Indiana and Kentucky, and Cincinnati Landmark Productions. Patrick has a background in theater, film, and television.

Chelsea Skalski was a last-minute decision to play the character of Ariana. I had already secured the role of another actress before pre-production even began. However, due to scheduling conflicts, she was not able to join the film. This was my biggest problem because the chemistry between the two leads had to be believable to make the film work.

My executive producer Herschel recommended the very talented Chelsea Skalski who proved to me that she was gifted by masterfully making the character her own. This was a "Happy Accident" that the role was recast.

Josh Schiller sculpted Herman the Penguin for the film and later helped to co-illustrate my two children's books. Josh is a close friend and creative partner. Josh operates Fishwood Inn, and his site is http://www.fishwoodinn.com.

Josh is a wild card of an artist doing animation, sculpting, and has even published his own children's book, *The Story of Little Pickle*.

Grace Guo my best friend and wife who inspired me to write this story. This film would not have been made if it were not for her. Her love, generosity, and support gave me the strength and courage to pursue this project to the end.

A special thanks to the rest of the cast and crew for all their hard work.

Every community across America is made up of a local artist trying to express themselves through some art form. I chose filmmaking, which is not a cheap art form to express oneself.

For Sale By Owner was made with a low budget and everyone on this film worked for free. I am truly grateful to every person that participated in this film with me.

I believe that we have made something unique and something meaningful. As an artist, I must entertain and enlighten audiences with material that will hopefully provoke emotion and inspire greatness within. It has been a privilege and an honor to work with my entire cast and crew. This was my first film, but hopefully not my last.

I would like to thank my family and my friends for their continuing support.

I would like to thank to my brother, Brian, my sister-in-law Jenifer, and my three nephews Jacob, Nick, and Luke.

Keith Barnett Huff

Louisville, KY

December 31, 2020

NEXT PAGE *PUBLISHERS*
LOUISVILLE, KY
EST. 2018 ™

FOR MORE EXCITING BOOKS
& UPCOMING EVENTS, VISIT US AT
WWW.NEXTPAGEPUBLISHERS.COM

Another Great Story
From the Author *of*
FOR SALE BY OWNER

HERMAN THE PENGUIN

By Keith Barnett Huff

What does it take to be a good penguin parent? Find out in this new children's story from the author of *Do Kangaroos Swim?* & *For Sale By Owner!*

A children's spin-off from the short story, *For Sale By Owner*.

Now Available!

The
Flower
is
Neutral

A Poetry Book
By Keith Barnett Huff

With additional poems by
Grace Guo & Ridley Barnett

Now Available

TWO STEPS
FROM HELL
ORIGINAL SCREENPLAY

A FRIGHTNING AND POWERFUL TALE of One Man's Journey Through the Afterlife!

The Henu Bark Express, a locomotive that transports the recently deceased, crosses the Duat to deliver its travelers to their final destination.

John Phoenix awakes on board the macabre train, unaware that he is dead, and discovers he is bound for Perdition. Jumping from the train, John journeys to find clues to his past. Along the way, he must evade the Medjay, guardians of the Netherworld, and demons that demand his help.

If John succeeds, will he escape with a new life or be damned forever in the fiery pits of Hell?

Also by
RIDLEY BARNETT

SPRING-HEELED JACK -or-
THE TERROR OF LOUISVILLE PART I

BASED ON TRUE EVENTS

An English Legend

July 28th, 1880. A mysterious flying ship enters the sky above Louisville, Kentucky. Spring-heeled Jack, a demon leaper of legend, arrives to terrorize the Derby City.

A Desperate Peace Officer

When religion plays a significant role in a man's career, William Quillo struggles to make the grade of detective because of his wife's Irish Catholic roots. But nothing will stop him from solving the mystery that is holding his city in awe.

A Secret Society

The Brotherhood of Khonsu, has an ungodly plan for Louisville. However, that plan is interrupted when Spring-heeled Jack steals the Brotherhood's sacred artifact. As they hunt for the demon leaper, William Quillo is caught in the middle of legend and un-holy rituals.

COMING JULY 28th, 2021

Read on for an excerpt from
SPRING-HEELD JACK or
THE TERROR OF LOUISVILLE Part I

July 28, 1880 – Wednesday

The Ohio River snakes and flows southwest past farmlands, forests, and cities small and large. Not long ago, it served as an extension of the Mason-Dixon Line that divided the U. S borders between free and slave territories. Six hundred miles down the Ohio from Pittsburgh is a twenty-six-foot drop known as the Falls of Ohio, the only obstruction to traffic on the river.

Located adjacent to the falls is the Portland Canal, where riverboats and barges are raised and lowered to bypass the vertical drop. High above the canal is the Pennsylvania Railroad Bridge, where a passenger train crosses south toward Kentucky. The train passes over narrow channels and exposed limestone ridges of the falls. Just before the treacherous drop, the river widens to a wharf, where steamboats sit moored to the shore, lining the riverbank, and would announce a city named in honor of King Louis XVI.

Louisville – the City of Progress - acts as a doorway to the west and gateway to the south. It is here, sprawled upon the south bank, a crowded, thriving metropolis of riches and poverty. In the shadows of its vast brick or stone mansions, tent towns huddled, and private clubs suitable for the wealthiest citizens were within a stone's throw of busy workhouses, where the truly desperate called home. As the business day ends, cyclists, mule-drawn buses, and horse-drawn carriages bustle up and down the packed brick and dirt streets of downtown Louisville.

Haddart's Apothecary, at the corner of Second Street and Chestnut - 6:28 P.M.

Two men sip their coffee at the rear third-floor window of the old drug store. C. A. Youngman, and Ben Flexner, pause to savor a gentle breeze after suffering the heat of yet another summer day. The moment of bliss is interrupted when Flexner's attention is caught by a large cigar-shaped object floating high above the Pennsylvania Railroad Bridge. "What is that?" he asks.

Youngman's eyes widen as he sees beyond Flexner's pointing finger. "Looks like a... toy balloon," he replies.

The swollen dirigible alters its course and drifts in their direction.

Looking to one another to verify if what they are seeing is real, the men hear a metal whirring sound that echoes across the city.

As the gas-filled airship nears a block away, the two men make out a propeller in its rear. Suspended under the top cigar-shaped portion is a vessel made of white steel, shaped like the keel of a ship, and a pilot surrounded by machinery. The aeronaut, dressed in black leather with a silver helmet and goggles, uses his hands and feet to control the rotating mechanism that gives the pilot control over the ship. The aeronaut is seated yet exerts himself to keep the balloon in a horizontal position by swinging his arms to and fro above his head as his feet work double treadles.

The sky is blotted out as the hulking cigar drifts overhead.

A second passenger materializes from a rear portion of the steel gondola. Dressed in the same attire, the man leans out to salute the two terrified men.

ABOUT THE AUTHOR

Keith Barnett Huff studies at Harvard University, focusing on earning his Master of Liberal Arts degree in Extension Studies, field: Creative Writing and Literature. Keith is the winner of the *Courier-Journal's* Young Authors Award for his children's book, *The Baby Turtle and Kangaroo*. He also wrote, produced, and directed the short film, *For Sale By Owner*. He was born in 1986 in Louisville and lives there now with his wife, *Grace*.